D0350017

Sports Illustrated KIDS

STARTING LINE READERS

Basketball BREAK

BY CC JOVEN
ART BY ÀLEX LÓPEZ

STONE ARCH BOOKS

a capstone imprint

Sports Illustrated Kids Starting Line Readers
is published by Stone Arch Books, a Capstone imprint
1710 Roe Crest Drive
North Mankato, Minnesota 56003
www.mycapstone.com

Copyright © 2017 by Stone Arch Books
All rights reserved. No part of this publication may be reproduced
in whole or in part, or stored in a retrieval system, or transmitted
in any formor by any means, electronic, mechanical, photocopying,
recording, or otherwise, without written permission of the publisher.

Sports Illustrated Kids is a trademark of Time Inc.
Used with permission.

Library of Congress Cataloging-in-Publication data
is available on the Library of Congress website.

ISBN: 978-1-4965-4253-3 (library binding)
ISBN: 978-1-4965-4260-1 (paperback)
ISBN: 978-1-4965-4264-9 (eBook pdf)

Summary: Lucas likes basketball, but he is a ball hog.
Can Lucas learn to pass the ball?

Printed in the United States of America
010056S17

This is Lucas.

Lucas likes basketball.

He likes to dribble.

He likes to shoot.

He shoots all the time.

Lucas is far from the basket.

He does not pass.

Lucas shoots.

His friend is open.
Lucas does not pass.

Lucas shoots.

Lucas cannot see the basket.

He does not pass.

Lucas shoots.

His coach is not happy.

His team is not happy.

Lucas takes a break.

Lucas watches.

His friends pass the ball.

Lucas goes back in.

Lucas passes the ball!

His team scores!

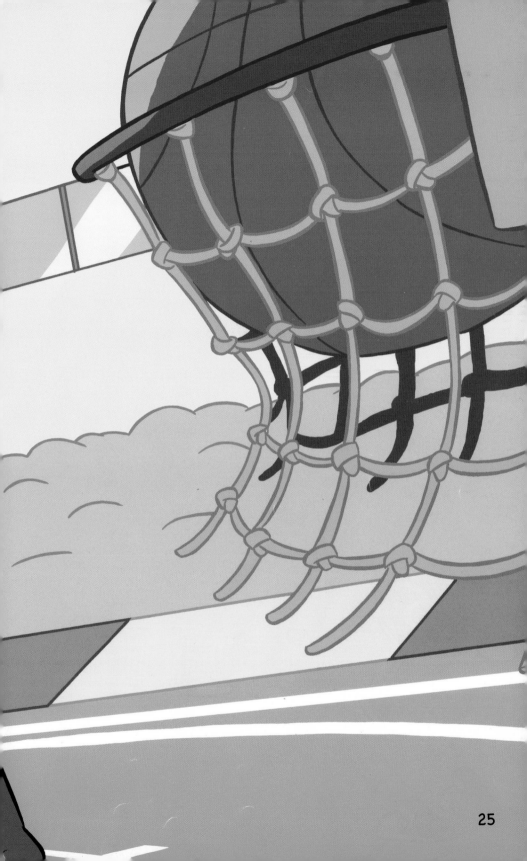

The team is happy.

The coach is happy.

Lucas is happy.

Lucas really likes basketball.

BASKETBALL
WORD LIST

basket

coach

dribble

pass

scores

shoot

team

word
count: 99

CONTRA COSTA COUNTY LIBRARY

31901060857739